76818

How the Devil
Gets His Due

ADAPTED AND ILLUSTRATED BY

Harold Berson

Crown Publishers, Inc.   New York

Printed in the United States of America

Library of Congress Catalog Card Number: 79-185085

Published simultaneously in Canada by General Publishing Company Limited

First Edition

The text of this book is set in 14 Pt. Univers 46
The illustrations are 3-color line and halftone illustrations

Once upon a time the devil bought himself an old broken-down castle. He had been driven from the city and wanted to live in the country where no one would know his true identity. The castle was surrounded by woods, farmland, meadows, and a fine old vineyard which the devil adored.

Now the devil
was very concerned
with appearances,
and after moving
his many fine clothes
into the castle,
he began putting
his lands in order.

Cutting wood,

pitching hay,

feeding the animals,
cleaning the stables,

harvesting the grapes,

weeding the vegetable garden,

repairing the roof,

and the floors,
and the doors,

and more and more.
The work was endless
and the devil soon grew tired
and irritable.
There was far too much work
and far too little pleasure,
so the devil began to make plans.

At the next village fair,
the devil made a bargain with a boy
who agreed to be his servant.
"Come and live with me in my castle
and help me take care of my lands.
But whoever complains, whether it is
you or I, will receive ten strong
blows with this stick."
And he held up a large knotted stick.
"I agree," said the boy, who was young
and strong and not suspicious by nature.

The devil sat by while his servant

stacked the hay,

fed the animals,

chopped the wood,

pulled the weeds
and tended the vineyard
from sunup to sundown
and beyond.
But the servant
dared not complain.

As the days went by,
he grew thinner
and thinner.
The devil, afraid
that his servant
would leave him,
told him to go home
for one week.
"Return rested
and strong," he said,
"for I shall never
find another like you."

The servant staggered home
and fell into the arms
of his horrified mother.
"I've done two months' work
in two weeks," he mumbled.
"I work from sunrise to
sunset without rest.
I've trimmed hedges,
mended fences,
repaired the roof,
harvested the grapes,
and should my master hear
me complain he will give me
ten whacks with his stick.
For that is our agreement."

"Let me take your place for one week,"
said his brother. "Your master will be
the one to complain when I am through,
even if he is the devil himself."

While the servant was away,
the devil had to look after the castle
and tend the lands alone.
The harder he worked,
the angrier he became.

He stomped and fumed,
he kicked and pulled at his beard.

And in his rage, he decided
he would work his servant until he was
no more than a bag of clacking bones.

The morning the servant was to return,
the devil was waiting impatiently at the gate.
"I have come to take the place of my brother,"
said the boy as he approached his new master.
"Very well," replied the devil,
"so long as you know the conditions."

"But before work one must eat,"
and the devil placed a loaf of bread
he had baked in front of his new servant.
And next to it he placed a soft-boiled egg.
"My friend, my dear, dear friend,"
began the devil, "you may eat all
of the bread that you can get inside
the yellow of this egg."

The new servant broke the egg
into a bowl. Then he dipped a goose
quill into the yellow of the egg and
drew a line around the whole loaf.
"I must have all of the bread for myself,"
said the servant in an even voice.
"Are you not pleased?"

"Yes, I am pleased," cried the devil
who was taken by surprise.

The next morning, the devil
greeted his servant with smiles and sugary words.
"Did you sleep well, my dear boy?
...Ah, good....It's a cold gray day indeed.
Perhaps you would be so kind
as to collect a wagonload of wood
— use the large wagon, of course.
And collect only the most twisted and bent
pieces on my property. I'll accept no others."

The servant pulled the wagon to the gentle slope of the vineyard. Before him lay row after row of twisted woody vines which year after year produced marvelous fruit.

The servant pulled up each and every vine by the roots
and piled them into the wagon.

The devil pulled his hair and tore his clothes when he saw
what his new servant had done.
"But I have brought you the most twisted and bent pieces of wood
on your property, exactly what you wanted," said the servant.
"Are you not pleased?"
"Yes! I am pleased," cried the devil.

The devil thought about his
ruined vineyard all day,
and by evening he could
barely control his anger.
"Perhaps," he snarled, "you would
be kind enough to sew up all of
the holes in my clothes. You must
not miss a single one, and furthermore,
everything must be finished by morning."

"Nothing can go wrong,"
he thought as he went to bed.

The next morning, the devil got out of bed
and started to put on his clothes.
Impossible. Everything was sewn shut—armholes,
legholes, neckholes, buttonholes.
He ran to the closet and realized
that his orders had indeed been followed.
Every piece of clothing that he owned had been
sewn shut. Not even a buttonhole remained open.

"My clothes," cried the devil,
"what have you done?"
"Exactly what you asked," said the servant,
who was standing at the door.
"Are you not pleased?"

The devil paused and shook his head slowly.
"Yes," he replied quietly, "I am pleased.
You do everything I ask and more."

"And more?" asked the servant slyly.

"Yes," said the devil.
"Now my vineyard is ruined and my clothes…"

"Aha," shouted the servant,
"you are complaining."

And he picked up the devil's stick and beat him

until he ran howling from the castle and
was never seen in that part of the country again.

The next day the boy and his brother
and their parents moved into the castle
where they found pleasure
in cutting wood,
pitching hay,
feeding the animals,
and more and more.